CW00687211

ESTABLISHED 2021

This book is dedicated to:

My Dad, for bringing my ideas to life and for working with me on this book, it's been a dream come true.

To all of the children I have taught, for inspiring me to write something that I can share with all children I continue to teach.

To all soldiers, past and present, for your bravery and commitment.

And to you, the reader, for buying this book, raising money for the Royal British Legion, and for supporting my dream in becoming a children's author.

Thank you.

A Day To Remember

Written by Beth Eastham
Illustrated by Karl Eastham

Orla and her Mummy were in the supermarket.

Orla noticed lots of people wearing flowers on their clothes.

“Mummy, why are those people wearing flowers?” she asked.

“Now Orla, that is a very good question.

Before you were born, there was a war”, Mummy began to explain.

"What's a war?" Asked Orla.

"Now Orla, that is a very good question.

A war is when groups of people don't agree on something, and they decide to have a long battle that sometimes lasts many years.

Lots of people get hurt and it brings lots of sadness to many people" Mummy explains.

"It sounds scary Mummy", said Orla.

"I think it would have been very scary,
and upsetting for many people.
All of the soldiers who fought in the war were very brave"
shares Mummy.

“What does brave mean Mummy?” Orla asks.

“Now Orla, that is a very good question”, Mummy replies, “brave means that people are strong even when times are scary; they may be afraid but this doesn’t stop them, because they are courageous and they need to help others”.

"Like superheroes Mummy? Superheroes are brave to catch the bad guys that might hurt them" Orla exclaims.

"Exactly Orla, in fact, soldiers are real life superheroes!" Mummy says.

"*WOW!* I never knew that!" An excited Orla replies.

“Come on now Orla, let’s get this shopping in the car, Daddy will be wondering where we are”, Mummy says to Orla.

When they arrived home, Orla was curious to find out more about real life superheroes.

“Daddy, did you know that soldiers are real life superheroes??!” Orla asks.

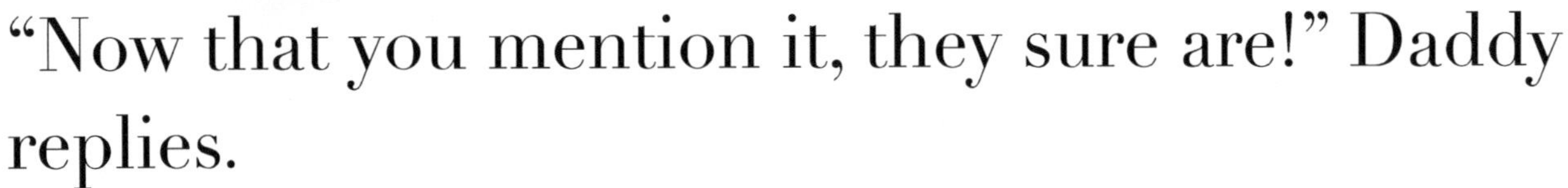

“Now that you mention it, they sure are!” Daddy replies.

“Mummy told me about the wars. But why do people wear flowers on their clothes?” Orla questions.

“Now Orla, that is a very good question”, Daddy says, “Were they wearing red and black flowers?” Daddy asks.

“Yes!” Orla replies, “How did you know that?” She asks inquisitively.

“Well, it’s nearly Remembrance Day, and people wear poppies - which are flowers that are mainly red with a black centre - to show they remember all of the soldiers”.

Orla listens to every word Daddy says. “But why poppies Daddy, is it because the soldiers like those type of flowers?” Orla asks.

“Now Orla, that is a very good question”, Daddy says, “people wear poppies as during one of the wars, the First World War, poppies often grew and flourished in the churned up soil.

This was because of all the fighting on the land. The poppies were pretty and brought some hope to the people, and now they are a symbol of these wars”.

Orla listened to every word, before asking "But Daddy, the people weren't wearing real poppies, they were pretend, why are they not wearing real poppies?".

“Now Orla, that is a very good question” Daddy says, “Years ago, people used to wear silk poppies. Silk is a soft material. But nowadays, we wear paper poppies, and do you know who makes them?” he asks.

Orla taps her chin, thinking really, really carefully. "Now Daddy, that is a very good question!" She exclaims.

Daddy smiles cheerfully, and then tells Orla "we don't wear real poppies because they need to be in the soil to grow, they won't grow if we wear them on our clothes. Some of the soldiers who used to fight in the wars now make the paper poppies, there are lots of factories set up to make them".

“Wow Daddy, that is so cool! So poppies are extra special aren’t they?! Special because we wear them to remember the real life superheroes, but super special because they are also made by the real life superheroes!

Please can I have one?” An excited, eager Orla asks.

Mummy overhears and walks into the kitchen. “Here you go Orla, I’ve got you one from the supermarket!”.

Orla’s face lights up the room.

“Thank you so much Mummy! I will wear it with pride!” Orla beams.

And from that day on, whenever Orla saw a soldier, an officer, or any other real life superhero, she thanked them for their bravery.

Beth Eastham is a Primary School Teacher from Lancashire.
She specialises in Early Years Education and has been teaching for the past 4 years.
This is the first book that she has written and published, with her Dad as illustrator.

Printed in Great Britain
by Amazon

29420774R00016